French Toast

Written by
Kari-Lynn Winters

Illustrated by
François Thisdale

pajamapress

First published in the United States in 2017
First published in Canada in 2016

Text copyright © 2016 Kari-Lynn Winters
Illustration copyright © 2016 François Thisdale
This edition copyright © 2016 Pajama Press Inc.
This is a first edition.

10 9 8 7 6 5 4 3 2 1

www.pajamapress.ca   info@pajamapress.ca

 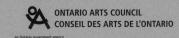

The publisher gratefully acknowledges the support of the Canada Council for the Arts and the Ontario Arts Council for its publishing program. We acknowledge the financial support of the Government of Canada through the Canada Book Fund (CBF) for our publishing activities.

Library and Archives Canada Cataloguing in Publication

Winters, Kari-Lynn, 1969-, author
        French toast / written by Kari-Lynn Winters ; illustrated by François Thisdale.
ISBN 978-1-77278-006-2 (hardback)
        I. Thisdale, François, 1964-, illustrator II. Title.
PS8645.I5745F74 2016   jC813'.6   C2016-902574-8

Publisher Cataloging-in-Publication Data (U.S.)

Names: Winters, Kari-Lynn, 1969-, author. | Thisdale, François, 1964-, illustrator.
Title: French Toast / written by Kari-Lynn Winters ; illustrated by François Thisdale.
Description: Toronto, Ontario Canada : Pajama Press, 2016. | Summary: "Pheobe, the daughter of a white French-Canadian mother and a Jamaican English-speaking father, dislikes her school nickname of "French Toast." Gently prompted by her blind grandmother, she uses descriptions of familiar foods from both cultures to explain the family's varied skin colors—and realizes she can take ownership of the nickname proudly"— Provided by publisher.
Identifiers: ISBN 978-1-77278-006-2 (hardcover)
Subjects: LCSH: Racially mixed people – Juvenile fiction. | Identity —Juvenile fiction. | Self-esteem – Juvenile fiction. | Grandmothers—Juvenile fiction. | BISAC: JUVENILE FICTION / Social Themes / Self-Esteem & Self-Reliance. | JUVENILE FICTION / Family / Multigenerational. | JUVENILE FICTION / Social Themes / Emigration & Immigration.
Classification: LCC PZ7.W568Fre | DDC [Fic] – dc23

Designed by Rebecca Bender

Manufactured by Friesens. Printed in Canada

Pajama Press Inc.
181 Carlaw Ave. Suite 207 Toronto, Ontario Canada, M4M 2S1

Distributed in Canada by UTP Distribution
5201 Dufferin Street Toronto, Ontario Canada, M3H 5T8

Distributed in the U.S. by Ingram Publisher Services
1 Ingram Blvd. La Vergne, TN 37086, USA

Original art created with digital media and acrylic

To two important girls in my life—my mom, Margaret, and my daughter, McKenna—K.W.

For my friend Giacomo—F.T.

Even though Nan-ma's blind,
she sees things others do not.

others do not.

On weekends, I am her neighborhood guide.

Today, I fall silent as we pass the school. I stare
at my sandals, wishing Nan-ma could walk faster.

Then one of the kids—the one who always carries
the basketball—shouts, "Hey, French Toast!"

Another kid laughs.

"Come on, Nan-ma," I say, pulling her. "The park is just up ahead..."

Near a bench, she stops me. "Do they call you that name because of your accent?"

If it were anyone else asking, I would yell, "*None of your business!*" But with Nan-ma, it's different.

I fidget with my zipper. "Um..."

She puts her hands on my face and I look into her foggy, blind eyes.

"And...maybe because of my...skin." My voice sounds uneven.

She nods. "Ahh, I see. I've never known the colors of skin. What color's yours?"

Her hands feel like warm banana leaves on my cheek.

"Um..." I say again, wishing my zipper would stop getting stuck.

"Phoebe?" she says, tilting her head slightly. "Your mind is as restless as a click beetle's nest."

So I make up an answer, "Like tea, after you've added the milk." And I hope that's all I have to say.

Nan-ma nods. "Warm and good."

I wonder about that. I don't always feel good. I don't feel good when strangers at the mall comment on my ringlets or ask me about my accent.

We keep walking. We pass the swing where, when I was younger, Ma pushed me to the moon—*la lune*, as she called it, and the teeter-totter where Pa turned me into a swallowtail butterfly and made me soar and dip in the sky.

I guide Nan-ma to the bench. We pass a kid from school. I don't know her name, but she smiles a lot.

"I've been told your mom is white," says Nan-ma.

I laugh. Not because Ma is so pale, but because white people really aren't white—not in the way that snow is white.

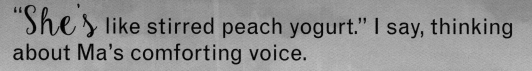

"She's like stirred peach yogurt." I say, thinking about Ma's comforting voice.

Nan-ma smiles. "Sweet, but also good."

I plunk down onto the bench. "Oui!" I say, trying make my voice sound smooth like Ma's. "The weather is so nice today—c'est magnifique!"

Nan-ma sits down too.

I wonder if talking about the weather will be enough to change the topic.

But Nan-ma sees more than most. "And your pa?"

"Like warm banana bread," I say.

"Mmm, reminds me of home."

I smile, knowing how great it is to bake Jamaican food with Pa. He's taught me how to make tamarind balls, ginger bulla, and sweet potato pudding.

"And what color am I?" she asks.

"Oh," I say, surprised. I wonder what it would be like to not know your own skin color? "You're like maple syrup, poured over..."

"...*Fr...Fren...*" I stop myself.

She finishes it for me. "French toast?"

I look away.

But Nan-ma closes her eyes and takes in a huge breath, as if she's noticed something yummy.

We sit in silence for a long time. I imagine the smells of breakfast and I think about the skin of those kids on the basketball court too—toasted coconut and cinnamon honey.

A Frisbee lands at my feet. The girl from school—her skin is like chocolate hazelnut spread—shouts, "over here!"

And I toss it back to her.

"Thanks, Phoebe!" she calls, waving.

She knows my name?

After a while, Nan-ma taps my leg, "I've never had colors explained in this way before."

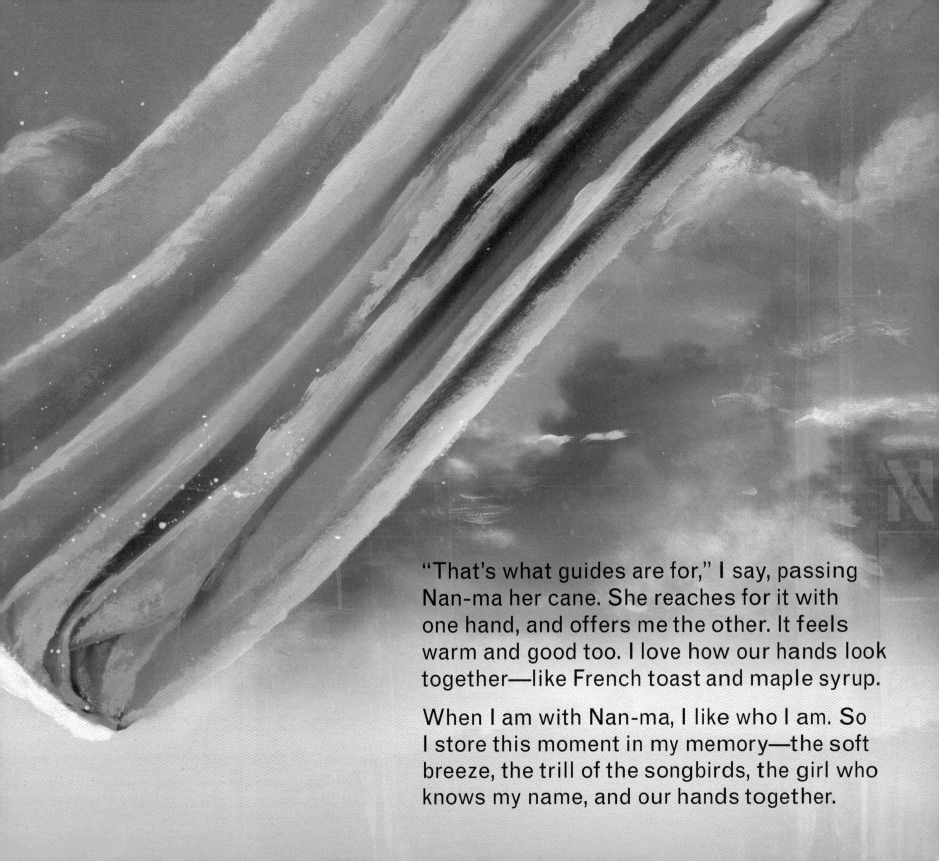

"That's what guides are for," I say, passing Nan-ma her cane. She reaches for it with one hand, and offers me the other. It feels warm and good too. I love how our hands look together—like French toast and maple syrup.

When I am with Nan-ma, I like who I am. So I store this moment in my memory—the soft breeze, the trill of the songbirds, the girl who knows my name, and our hands together.

"What will you have for breakfast, Sugar?" she asks as we pass the school.

This time I don't look at my feet. Instead, I look straight ahead and say quietly, "French toast."

Yes, I like the sound of that. "It's *French toast* for me!"